MR. MEN
in Scotland

Roger Hargreaves

Original concept by
Roger Hargreaves

Written and illustrated by
Adam Hargreaves

EGMONT

Mr Strong had always wanted to go to the Highland Games in Scotland.

He was going to compete in the caber tossing event. A sport that was ideally suited to Mr Strong as it was all about strength. Tossing a tree kind of strength.

He invited his friends to come too. They left a few days before the competition and planned to see the sights along the way.

Mr Strong had trouble packing his caber.

They all caught the train to Scotland. On their way to Edinburgh, they passed the Forth Bridge.

Little Miss Curious wondered what had happened to the First, the Second and the Third Bridges.

Mr Clever explained that it was named after the River Forth. Little Miss Curious thought for a moment.

"So what happened to the River First, the River Second and the River Third?" she asked.

Mr Clever sighed. It was going to be a very long day.

The next morning Mr Uppity went to wake Mr Lazy. "Get up!" he yelled. "We are going for a walk up the Royal Mile to see Edinburgh Castle!"

"A mile? I can't walk a mile!" cried Mr Lazy. And he turned over and went straight back to sleep.

Mr Uppity marched the others up the streets of the Royal Mile where they had a great view of the castle on its rock.

Mr Lazy also enjoyed a view of the castle …

… a view from his bed.

Through one eye.

One, half-closed, sleepy eye!

In the afternoon, Little Miss Splendid wanted to visit a woollen mill to find a sightseeing outfit.

She looked truly splendid in tartan.

Mr Rush wasn't really the right shape for a kilt.

And Mr Silly got in a tangle with his.

A tartan tangle!

The next day they drove to Glasgow to visit the Kelvingrove Art Gallery and Museum.

They saw so many things.

There was an elephant and an Egyptian mummy and paintings and sculptures and dinosaur skeletons and suits of armour and there was even an aeroplane hanging from the ceiling!

Mr Rush rushed round and saw everything.

Mr Lazy saw a lot less.

After exploring the gallery, Little Miss Greedy wanted to visit the cafe.

"You should try a haggis," suggested Mr Clever.

"What's a haggis?" asked Little Miss Greedy.

"It's a Scottish cow," said Mr Nonsense.

"No, no, no!" cried Mr Clever. "It's a food, like a giant sausage."

"A giant sausage?" said Mr Nonsense. "Don't be ridiculous!"

But of course, Mr Clever was right. And Little Miss Greedy enjoyed her haggis. And then she enjoyed another one. And another one!

It was time to head to the games. On the way, Little Miss Curious spotted a Highland cow.

"Now, that's a haggis!" announced Mr Nonsense.

Which was, of course, nonsense.

"It looks like a mini woolly mammoth," laughed Little Miss Sunshine. "It's as shaggy as Mr Clumsy. But not as clumsy!"

"Ow!" cried Mr Clumsy, who had sat on a thistle.

Mr Clever insisted on a quick stop at The St Andrews Golf Club, one of the oldest in the world.

"Scotland is the home of golf," announced Mr Clever.

Mr Clever knew an awful lot about the history of golf.

He knew an awful lot about the rules of golf.

There was only one thing he did not know about golf.

How to play!

There was one last place to visit before the games.

A very long lake called Loch Ness. It was even longer than Mr Tickle's arms. Which were as wiggly as Nessie, the Loch Ness Monster.

Many people think that Nessie is a Scottish myth and doesn't exist. But if that is true, then who is Mr Tickle tickling?

The next day they arrived at the Highland Games.

The games opened with a marching band of pipers and drummers.

Mr Noisy had never heard bagpipes before. He was very impressed.

Mr Quiet was not so impressed.

There were all sorts of games to watch. And all sorts of games to join in.

There was the Highland dancing competition for Little Miss Somersault.

There was the tug-o-war for Mr Greedy – nobody could move him!

And there was the hammer throw for Little Miss Dotty.

Although her hammer didn't count!

And then it was the caber tossing event.

Mr Strong's moment had arrived.

Mr Strong took a long run up and then, with all his might, he launched the caber into the air. It rose into the sky, tumbling end over end, and landed far down the field.

With a loud crack, it split in two.

Mr Strong had snapped his caber.

He was too strong!

Too strong, even for caber tossing.

Which made him the strongest man in the world.

Mr Strong was very pleased.

And then it was time to go home.

As the train pulled out of the station, there was a terrible noise from the back of the carriage.

"Oh help!" cried Mr Jelly, in terror. "The wheels have fallen off, the carriage has derailed, the train is going to crash!"

But it was none of these things.

It was Mr Noisy.

He had bought a souvenir.

Bagpipes!